Pilgrim's Progress

Written by
John Bunyan

story used from Pilgrim's Progress which were published by

MOODY PRESS -Chicago in 1952

Editors

Mrs. Sharon Muldoon (Grand Rapids, MI)
Mrs. Sally Rushmore (Carmel, IN)

illustrated by
James Tung

3/20/2011

Dedicated
To

UNHCR

United Nations High Commissioner For Refugees
in
Malaysia, Thailand and
Bethany Christian Service, Grand Rapids, Michigan
with all those who are laborering in humanitary work

PREFACE

John Bunyan (1628-1688) started writing this story in the prison amidst many experiences of trials and hardships in the world where he grew up. He was faced with religious persecution and imprisonment. He had four children. He married twice.

He wrote some other books, including his autobiography as well. He slept in the Lord just shortly before the religious persecution in England came to an end.

When a refugee artist read, his book, he felt as if he was seeing the same vision the author saw! As a matter of fact, he too, has experienced many kinds of hardships and trials both during the time he was raised by his grandmother and since that time. Even though the names of the locations the author and the artist visited may be different, they both fell into the same Slough of Despond.

Tung, the little refugee artist illustrated the vision of John Bunyan from his own Asian point of view. It is the sincere and honest desire of the artist that the hearts of every member of armed groups in this world, as well as anyone who can read a book, may be deeply touched by this book and come to know the Lord.

James Tung
(A Refugee From Myanmar)
September 4, 2010 Grand Rapids,
Michigan, The U.S.A

To order additional copies of this book, contact:
Xlibris Corporation
1-888-795-4274
www.Xlibris.com
Orders@Xlibris.com
90870

As I walked through the wilderness of this world,

I lighted on a certain place which was a den, and I lay down in that place to sleep. As I slept, I dreamed a dream.

1

The Pilgrim's Progress

I saw a man clothed with rags standing with his face turned away from his own house,

He opened the book and read it very seriously.

a book in his hand and a great burden upon his back.

As he read, he broke out with a lament, saying,

What shall I do?

He could not be silent long because his trouble increased.

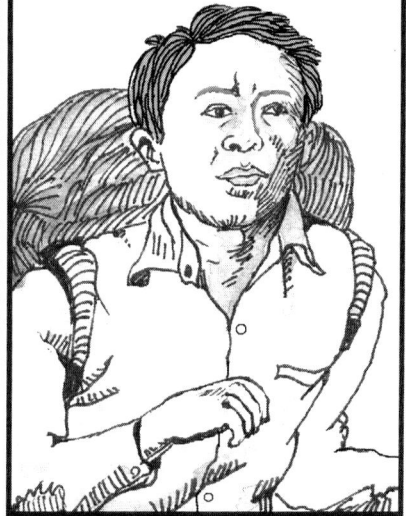

He began to talk to his wife and children again as to what the book warned about.

My dear wife and children, I have a very big burden upon my back.

Our city will be burnt with fire and brimstone from heaven one day.

We will all perish unless some way of escape can be found whereby we may be delivered.

His wife and the children thought that some foolish ideas got into his head and that he had gone crazy. They hoped sleep might settle his brains, so with all haste they got him to bed.

He spent the night in sighs and tears. When the morning came, his condition was worse.
He tried to talk to them again.

But they attempted to drive away his fear by being mean to him.

Sometimes they would deride, sometimes they would chide,

and sometimes they would just neglect him.

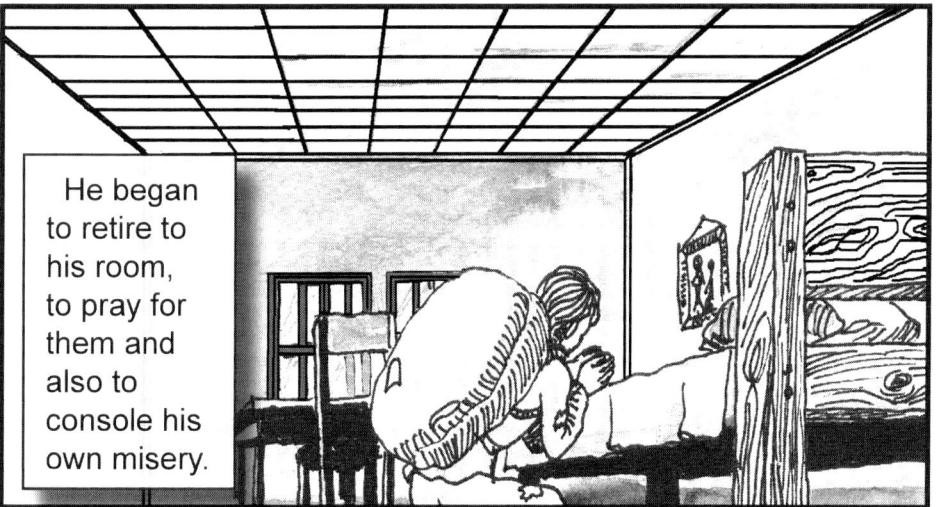

He began to retire to his room, to pray for them and also to console his own misery.

5

He would walk in the field alone.

Sometimes reading and sometimes praying.

For some days he spent his time in that way.

He was greatly distressed in his mind as he read. He burst out crying:

What must I do to be saved?

He looked this way and that way as if he would run, yet he stood still because he was not sure which way to go.

Then, in my dream I saw a man named Evangelist come to him and ask him:

Why are you crying?

"Sir, I realize that I am condemned to die, and after that to come to judgment. I find that I am not willing to do the first, nor able to do the second."

Why are you not willing to die, since this life is filled with so many evils?

Because I fear that this burden on my back will make me sink lower than the grave and I shall fall into the hell. If I am not fit to go to prison,

I am not fit to go to judgment and from thence to executions.

If this is your condition, why do you stand still?

Because I don't know where to go.

Then Evangelist gave him a parchment roll, in which was written, *"Flee from the wrath to come."* **Matt. 3:7**

Where must I flee?

The man read it and asked Evangelist;

Do you see the gate over there?

No.

LIFE! LIFE! LIFE!
Luke 14:26

Without looking back, he ran toward the middle of the plain. Gen. 19:17

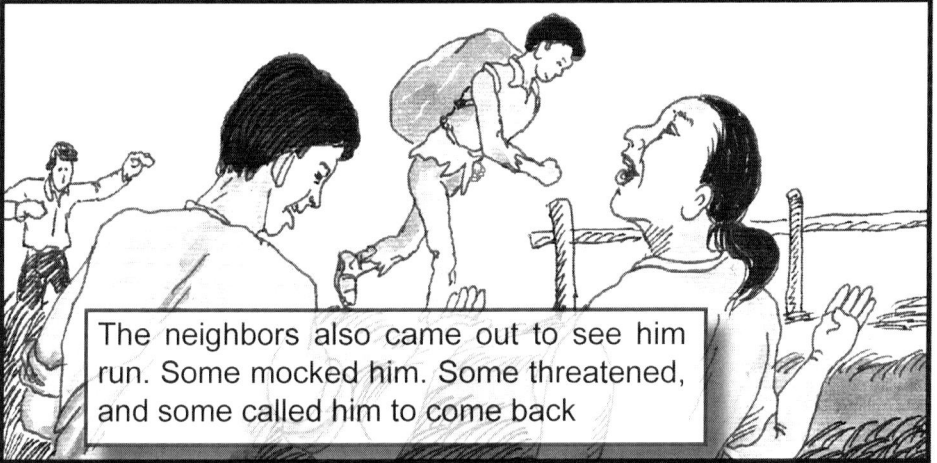

The neighbors also came out to see him run. Some mocked him. Some threatened, and some called him to come back

Two neighbors, Obstinate and Pliable, wanted to bring him back by force.

Panel 1: But by then the man was a good distance from them. However, in a little time, they overtook him.

Panel 2: Neighbors, why did you come?

To persuade you to go back with us.

Panel 3: That's impossible! You live in the city of Destruction where I was also born.

Sooner or later, you will sink lower than the grave into a place that burns with fire. Be content, friends, and go along with me.

What? You want us to go with you! And leave our friends and our comforts behind us!

"Yes." said Christian, for that was his name.

II Corin. 4:18

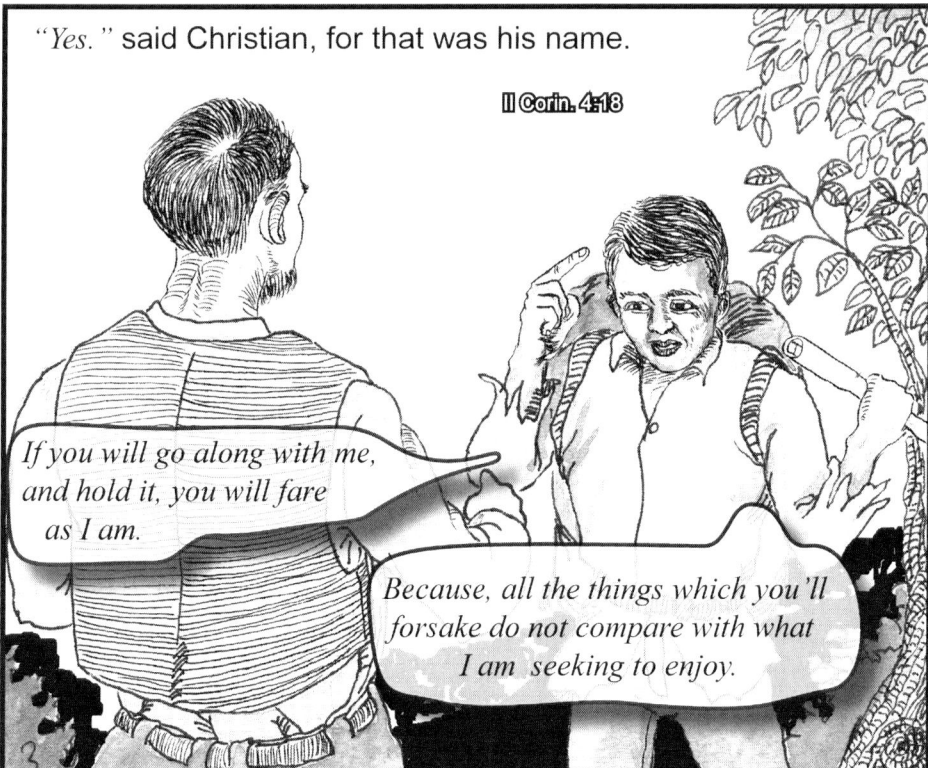

If you will go along with me, and hold it, you will fare as I am.

Because, all the things which you'll forsake do not compare with what I am seeking to enjoy.

14

Luke 9:62
No, I won't, because I have laid my hands to the plow.
Come then, Pliable. Let's go home without him.
There is a company of these crazy headed coxcombs, that when they take a fancy by the end, are wiser in their own eyes than seven men that can render a reason.
Then don't hate. If what the good Christian says is true, the things he seeks are better than ours. My heart inclines to go with my neighbor.

16

17

I'd better go back to my place alone.

Come then, good neighbor, let's get going.

Then they both went together.

Obstinate went back home. Christian and Pliable went talking on the plain, and thus they began their discourse.

Please tell me more details about what the things are, how they are to be enjoyed and to where we are going.

I can better conceive of them with my mind than speak of them with my tongue.

19

There are crowns of glory to be given to us, and garments that will make us shine like the sun. There shall be no more crying or sorrow, for the owner of the place will wipe all tears from our eyes.

Matt 13:43
Rev. 7:17, 17; 21:4

Rev. 4:4;
14:1-5

There we shall meet with ten thousand that have gone before us to that place. None of them are hurtful, but loving and holy. We shall see the elders with their golden crowns, and the holy virgins with their golden harps.

There we shall see men that by the world were cut in pieces, burned in flames, eaten by beasts and drowned in the sea because of the love they bore to the Lord of the place, all well, and clothed with immortality as with a garment II Cor. 5:2,3,5; John 12:25

Isa. 55:1,2; John 6:37; Rev. 22:17

What shall we do to share this?

The Lord of that country has recorded that in this book. If we are truly willing to have it, He will bestow it upon us freely.

21

I am glad to hear of these things. Come on, let's walk faster.
I cannot go as fast as I want, because of the burden on my back.

Now I saw in my dream that they drew near to a bog that was in the middle of the plain.

The Slough of Despond

Because they were not paying attention, they both suddenly fell into the bog. The name of the Slough was Despond. Here, they had to wallow in the mud for a long time.

And Christian, because of the burden on his back, began to sink in the mire.

Ah, neighbor Christian, where are you now?

I really don't know.

At this Pliable began to be offended, and angrily said to his fellow.

Is this the happiness you have told me of? If we have such ill speed at our first setting out, what may we expect between this and our journey's end?

If I get out of this trouble alive, you may possess the brave country alone for me.

He gave a desperate struggle or two, and got out of the mire on that side of the Slough which was nearest to his own house.

So he went away and Christian saw him no more.

Christian was left to struggle in the Slough of Despond alone, but he still endeavored to struggle to the side that was far from his house and next to the gate.

But he could not get out of the Despond because of the burden on his back.

HELP COME to THE RESCUE
What are you doing here?
Meanwhile a man named Help came to him and asked;

Sir, I was bid to go this way by Evangelist. He directed me to go to the gate over there so that I might escape from the wrath to come.

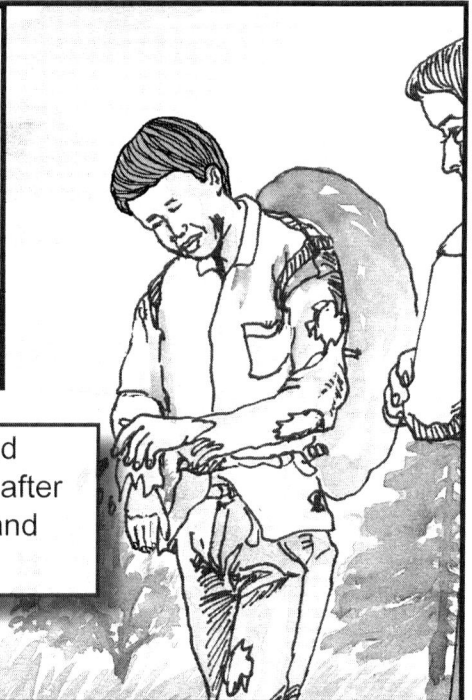

Then I stepped to Mr. Help who plucked out Christian and said,

Sir, Why, since this place is the way from the city of Destruction to yonder gate, is it that this place is not mended, that poor travelers might go there with more security?

This miry Slough cannot be mended. It is called the Slough of Despond, because it is where scum and filt that accompanies conviction of sin.

As the sinner is awakened about his lost condition, there arise in his soul many fears and doubts and discouraging apprehensions,

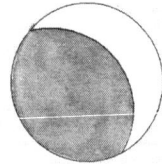

which settle in this place. And this is the reason of the badness of this ground.

Isa. 35:3,4

It is not the pleasure of the King that this place should remain so bad.

Sorry, the gun triggered off itself and killed the kid without intention.

His laborers have been, for about these two thousand years employed about this ground, and it should have been mended.

Say, they are the best materials to make good ground of this place. However, it is still the Slough of Despond

Eph. 2:19-22

and so it will be when they have done what they can.

True, there are, by the directions of the lawgiver, very good and substantial steps placed throughout this Slough.

But, at this time, this place continues to spew out its filth, no matter what the weather is. So these steps are hardly seen.

Men, through the dizziness of their heads, step besides, and then they are bemired in their purpose, even though there are steps.

Anyway, the ground will be good once you get in at the gate.

By then, Pliable was home and his neighbors came to visit him, and were entertained by his stories upon his return.

Christian Meets With Mr. Worldly Wiseman

Now, as Christian was walking by himself, he saw a man afar off coming across the field in his direction. The name of that man was Mr. Worldly Wiseman.

News about Christian had spread across the country.

He dwelt in the town of Carnal Policy, which was a very great town, close to where Christian lived.

Mr. Worldly Wiseman had some opinions about Christian. By observing his sighs and groams, . and the like, he struck up a conversation with Christian.

Hi friend, where are you going with this great burden?

I am going to the gate over there beyond this field.

When I get there, I will be shown a way to get rid of this heavy burden.

Do you have a wife and children?

Yes, I do. But I can no more take pleasure in them as I did in the earlier times because of this burden.

Now I feel like being single.

I Cor. 7:29.

Will you listen to me if I give you some advice?

If it's good, I will, for I am in need of good counsel.

You will never get rid of this burden in this way.

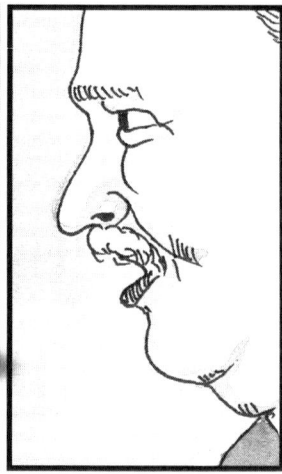

As long as your mind is un-settled you can not enjoy the benefits of the blessings which God has bestowed upon you.

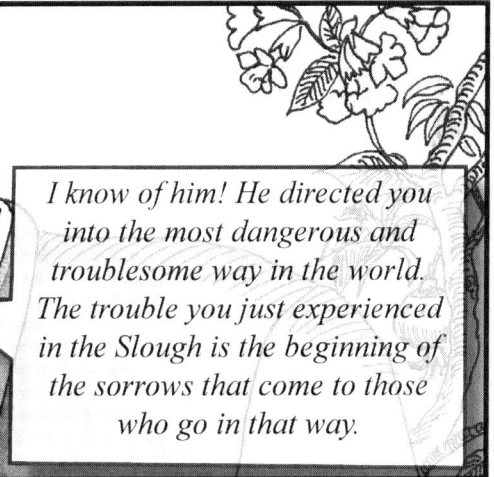

Listen to me. In the way which you go, there are troubles:

pain, hunger, perils, sword, lions, dragons, darkness and death. Why should a man so carelessly cast away himself by listening to a stranger?

Because sir, this burden upon my back is more terrible to me than all those things

which you've mentioned.

I won't care about them if I am just going to meet with deliverance from my burden.

How did you get this burden at first?

By reading this book.

Well, the remedy is at hand. You don't have to go on this troublesome, dangerous way. I can direct you to obtain what you desire most. Instead of those dangers, you shall meet with much safety, friendship and satisfaction.

Sir, please open this secret to me.

The village over there is named Morality. There dwells a judicious man whose name is Legality.

He has skills to cure those who are crazy in their wits with their burdens. His house is not quite a mile from this place.

Mr. Civility, son of Legality, also can do it to you! You can send for your wife and children,

and live in this village peacefully and happily the rest of your whole life.

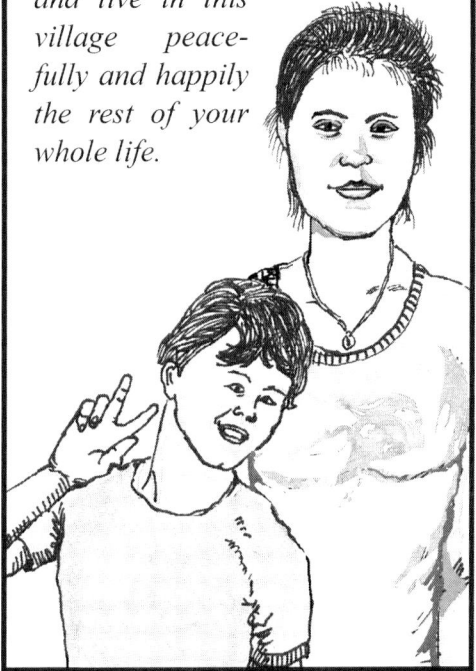

There are houses now standing empty, one of which you may have for a reasonable price. Provision there also is cheap and good.

You will live by honest neighbors, in credit and good fashion.

If what this gentleman has said is true, I'd better take his advice.

Sir, how do I get to this honest man's house?

Do you see the hill over there?

Yes, I do.

Toward that hill you must go. The first home you come to is his home.

Thus, Christian turned out of his way to go to Mr. Legality's house.

When he got near the hill, it seemed so high, so steep that Christian was afraid to venture further.

Lest the hill should fall on his head, he stood still at the food of the hill.

Now he didn't know what to do. Also his burden now seemed heavier to him than while he was on his way.

There came flashes of fire and smoke out of the hill

Heb. 12:21

Therefore, he did sweat and tremble with fear. Exo. 19:16, 18

41

Now he began to feel sorry that he had taken Mr. Worldly Wiseman's counsel. Meanwhile, he saw Evangelist coming toward the place where he was standing.

He began to blush for shame.

Evangelist came up to him.

He looked upon him with a severe and dreadful countenance.

What are you doing here?

But I said I was so laden with the burden which is on my back, that I can not take pleasure in them as formerly.

And I told him where I was going and the reason for going there...

and everything in detail.

Then he said that he would show me a better way, which was a short cut as well.

Thus, I was on my way to that gentle man's house, the gentleman who was said to have the skills to take off this burden.

But now as you see, how high and steep the hill is that I am supposed to climb! It's too dangerous to climb up this hill. I don't know what shall I do.

Stand still for a while that I may teach you the words of God.

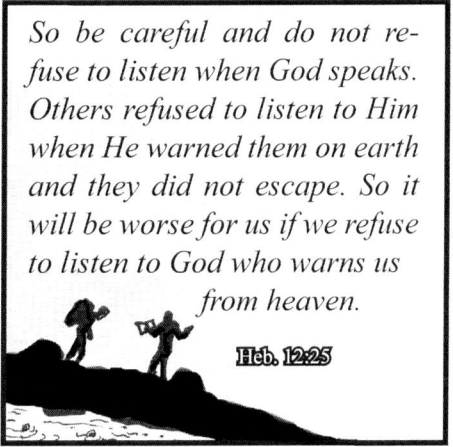

So be careful and do not refuse to listen when God speaks. Others refused to listen to Him when He warned them on earth and they did not escape. So it will be worse for us if we refuse to listen to God who warns us from heaven.

Heb. 12:25

Those who are right with me will live by faith. But if they turn back with fear, I will not be pleased with them.

You are the man who is running into misery. You've begun to reject the counsel of the most high.

You drew back your foot from the way of peace, even almost to the hazarding of your own damnation.

49

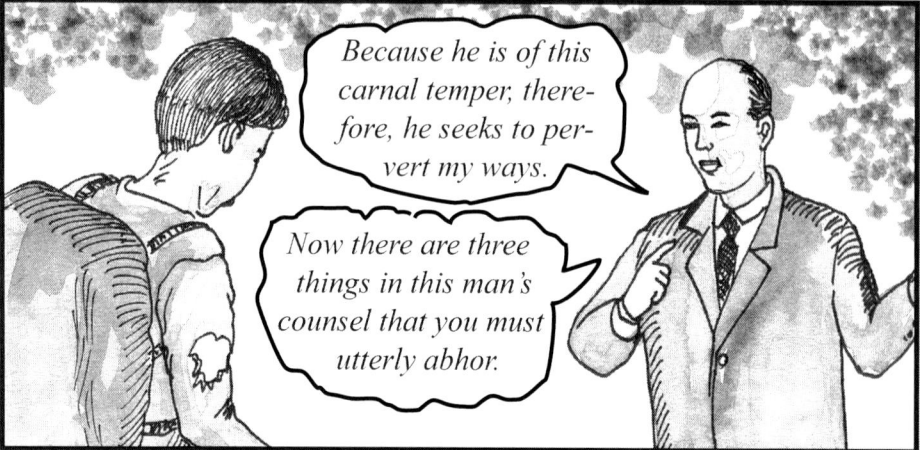

Heed earnestly to the thing I will tell you of.
The man you encountered was a Worldly Wiseman. They savor only of the doctrine of this world. They love that doctrine best, for it saves them from the cross.
1 John. 4:5, Gal. 6:12

Because he is of this carnal temper, therefore, he seeks to pervert my ways.

Now there are three things in this man's counsel that you must utterly abhor.

His turning you out of the way,

Luke 13:24

his laboring to render the Cross odious to you, and

Heb. 11:25, 26

his setting your feet in the way that leads unto death.

He to whom you were sent, was named Legality. He's the son of the bondwoman, who is in bondage with her children. How can you expect by them to be made free? Gal. 4:21-27

50

You cannot be justified by the works of the law. For by deeds of the law no man living can be rid of his burden.

Therefore... Mr. Worldly Wiseman is an alien.

Mr. Legality is a cheat.

legality

Law

Cult-ure

His son Civility, with his simpering looks, is but a hypocrite.

Evangelist called aloud to the heavens for confirmation of what he had said. And there came words and fire out of the hill.

"But those who depend on following the law to make them, right are under a curse, for it is written, Gal. 3:10

Anyone will be cursed who does not always obey what is written in the book of the law."

Now Christian cried out with a great lament, cursing the time he met with Mr. Worldly Wiseman. And he was also greatly ashamed of his behavior; forsaking the right way, and following only from the flesh.

Sir, is there any hope for me? May I now go back and go up to the gate?

I am so sorry I have listened to that man's counsel. But may my sin be forgiven?

You've committed two evils. You've forsaken the way that's good to tread the forbidden path. Yet the good man at the gate will accept you. Only keep in mind and take heed that you won't turn aside again, lest you perish from the way.

And Evangelist gave him a kiss and said goodbye.

Thank you so much sir. Good bye!

Good bye.

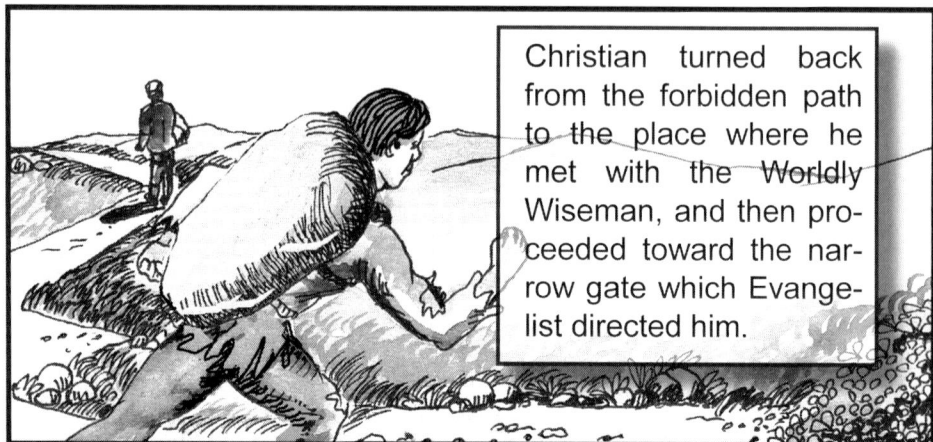

Christian turned back from the forbidden path to the place where he met with the Worldly Wiseman, and then proceeded toward the narrow gate which Evangelist directed him.

On the door was written; *Knock, and it shall be opened unto you.*

Matt. 7:7

May I now enter here? Will he within open to forgive me, though I have been an undeserving rebel? Then shall I not fail to sing His lasting praise on high.

Knock, knock.

At last, there came a solemn person to the gate, named Goodwill.

Who are you? Where are you from? What do you want?

I am a poor burdened sinner. I come from the city of Destruction, but I'm going to mount Zion,

that I maybe delivered from the wrath to come. I am informed that by this gate is the way to there.

And also some of my neighbors stood crying and calling after me to return. But I put my fingers in my ears, and so came on my way.

Did anyone of them follow you to persuade you to go back?

He told them about Pliable and Obstinate in detail.

Oh my! What a poor man!

Is the celestial glory of so little esteem with him that he counted it not worth running the hazard of a few difficulties to obtain it?

And Christian also told them about meeting with Mr. Worldly Wiseman and then going toward Mr. Legality's house.

The hill has been the death of many, and will be the death of many more. It was good that you escaped from getting dashed to pieces.

I don't know what would have become of me there if merciful God didn't send Evangelist to me again.

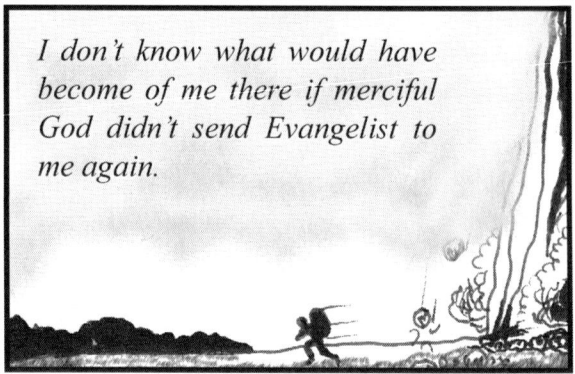

Christian paused speaking for a moment, took a deep breath, and then continued his confession.

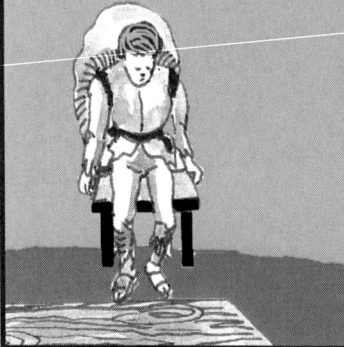

What a favor is this to me, who is fit indeed for death by that mountain, that instead I sit talking with my Lord.

We make no objections against people whatever they have done before they come here. They are not cast out.
John 6:37
Look at the narrow way before you. It was the way that the patriarchs, prophets, Christ and his apostles walked. It is as straight as a rule can make it.
This is the way you must go.

For, there it will fall from your back itself.

After awhile, Christian got up and set out on his journey again.

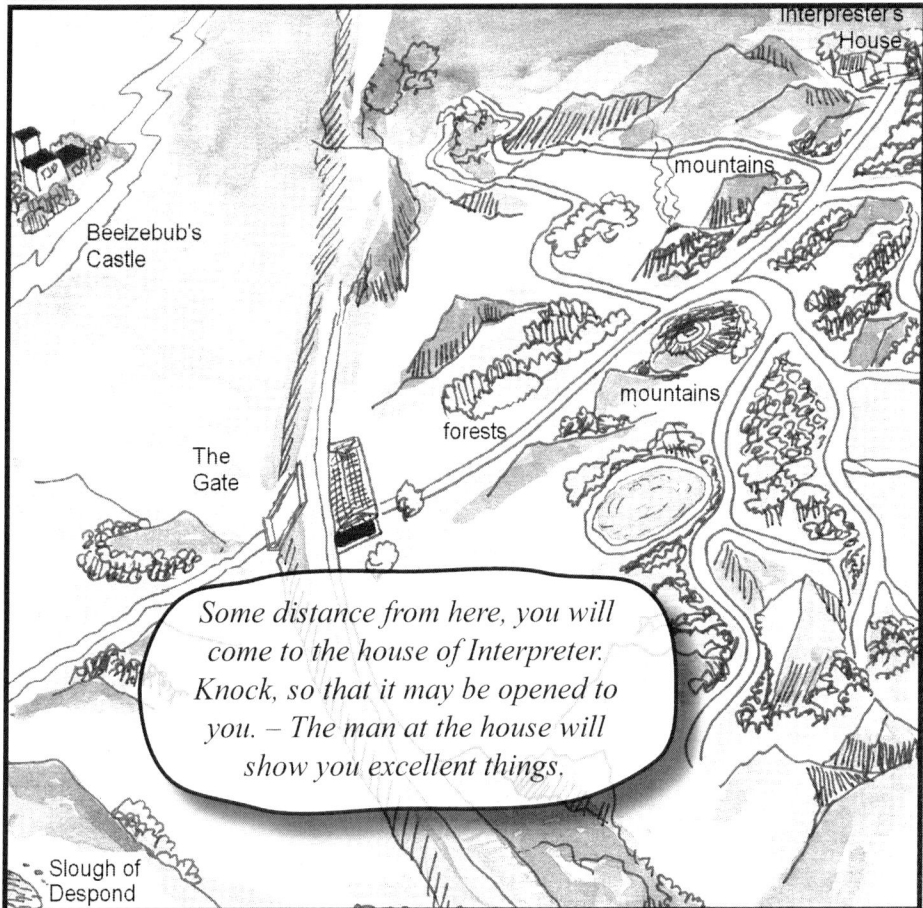

Interprester's House

mountains

Beelzebub's Castle

mountains

forests

The Gate

Some distance from here, you will come to the house of Interpreter. Knock, so that it may be opened to you. – The man at the house will show you excellent things.

Slough of Despond

House of the Interpreter

I am a traveler who was bid by a friend of the owner of this house. I would like to speak with the master of this house.

She made him wait outside the main building and went back inside to call the master of the house to welcome him.

After a little while, the master of the house, so called Interpreter came to see him. He asked him what he would like to have.

Sir, I am from the city of Destruction, and am on my way to Mount Zion..

I need you to show me excellent things, such as would be helpful to me in my journey.

Come in, I will show you things that will be profitable to you.

He was led into a private room.

He had his man light the candles.

Light the candles and open the door.

There on the wall, was hung up a picture of a very quiet and serious looking man in appearance.

Inside The Private Room.

66

He had eyes lifted up to heaven, .

the world was behind his back.

The best of books in his hand, and

What does this mean?

He was just one of a thousand.

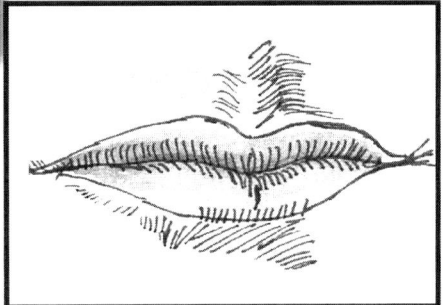

the law of the truth is written on his lips. It is to show you that his work is to know and unfold dark things to sinners.

Teaching Inside the Private Room

He can speak in the words of the apostle. He said; "Although you may have ten thousand teachers in Christ, you do not have many fathers. Through the good news I became your father in Christ Jesus."

1 Cor. 4:15

There is a crown on his head. That is to show you that slighting and despising things that are present, for the love that he has to his master's service, he is sure of his reward and glory in the next life.

Gal. 4:19

"My little children, again I feel the pain of childbirth for you until you truly become like Christ".

He is the only authorized person of God who stands as your guide in all difficult places and situations.

A Very Large Parlor

Then he took him by the hand and led him into a very large living room that was full of dust.

He commanded, "Sweep the room please."

As the servant began to sweep the room, the dust started to fly abundantly about as the room had never been swept.

"Bring water and sprinkle the room."

So did she, and now the room was cleansed.

70

The gospel comes as a sweet and precious influence to the heart. Then the sin is vanquished and subdued, and the soul made clean, through the faith of it, and consequently fit for the king of glory to inhabit.

John 15:3, Eph. 5:26, Rom. 16:25

Let's go into another room. Come, please.

Yes

Interpreter led him into a small room where two little boys were sitting.

Passion and Patience

The name of the eldest boy was Passion, and the younger one's name, Patience.

Passion seemed to be much discontented. Patience was very quiet.

The boys' tutor wanted them to wait for their best things till the beginning of next year. But Passion wanted to have his portion right now.

Patience, his younger brother was willing to wait.

Then I saw that a man came to Passion, and brought him a sack of treasures and poured it down at his feet

Passion laughed at Patience to scorn him.

He took all his treasures and went to live it up.

But within a while, he had squandered it all away, and had nothing left but rags.

Passion had no reason to laugh at Patience that much because Luke 16:25

Patience will have everlasting treasure and glory like Lazarus did.

Then I perceive that it is not to covet things that are temporary and perishable, but to wait for things to come.

You are right, for things that are seen are *temporary*, but the things that are not seen last eternally. II Corin. 4:18

Interpreter took Christian by the hand and led him into a place where a fire was burning against a wall.

The fire is the work of grace that is wrought in the heart. Devil cast water upon it in order to put it out.

There is another man on the other side of the wall. He filled the fire place up with more oil (grace) continuously. He is Christ, the Lord.

That's the reason why the fire burns higher and hotter.

II Corin. 12:9

God's grace is enough for man. When he is weak, His power is made perfect in him.

This is to teach you that it is hard for the tempted to see how this work of grace is maintained in the soul.

Then Interpreter led him to a pleasant place where a stately palace was built. Christian was greatly delighted to see that beautiful palace

Certain persons who were clothed all in gold were also seen walking inside the palace.

There were many people who wanted to go inside, waiting outside the door.

May I go inside?

No. We can go closer and watch them.

However, they could not go inside freely because there was a man sitting at a table by the door who takes the name of him that should enter therein.

And also there stood many soldiers in armor guarding the door and protecting from illegal trespassers.

Then Christian saw a man of a very stout countenance come up to the table and say;

Set down my name, please.

Now the man put a helmet upon his head, drew his sword,

and rushed toward the door, upon the guard.

Like a thunder storm, he fought againt those guards.

So after he had received and given many wounds to those that attempted to keep him out, he cut his way through them all, and passed forward into the palace.

Matt. 11:12, Acts. 14:22

And there was a pleasant voice heard from those that were within, even of those that walked upon the top of the palace saying:

Come in. Come in, eternal glory thou shall win.

I think I understand the meaning of this.

DESPAIR
Now let me go hence.
No, I still have to show you a little more. After that you'll go on your way.
Come, come in
In a very dark room, a man was sitting in an iron cage. He looked very sad.
His eyes were looking down to the ground and he sighed as if he would break his heart.
What are you?

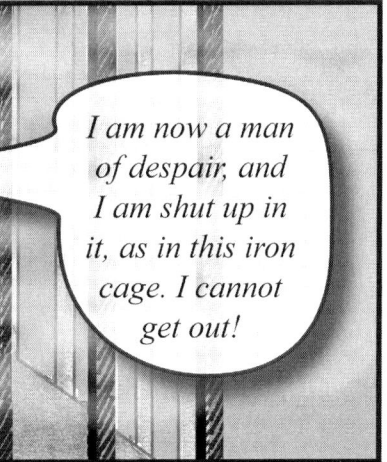

How did you come into this condition?

I laid the reins upon the neck of my lust. I sinned a lot and had grieved the Holy Spirit. Now He's gone.

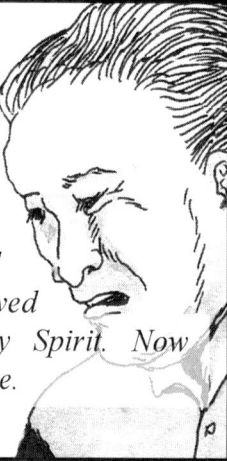

I tempted the devil, and he has come to me. Now God has left me.

becoming a member of the Harlot of Babylon.

becoming a member of the Harlot of Babylon.

I have so hardened my heart that I cannot repent.

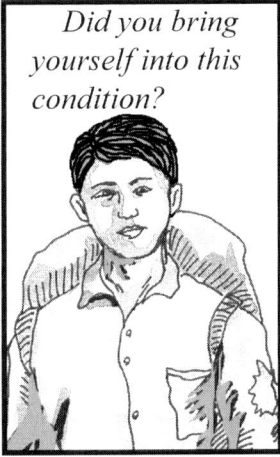

Did you bring yourself into this condition?

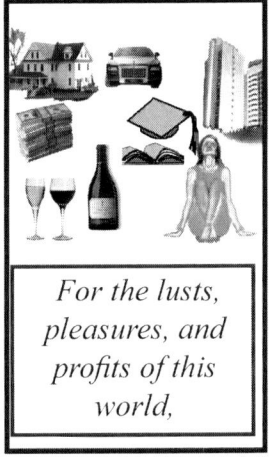

For the lusts, pleasures, and profits of this world,

but now every one of those things also bites me, and gnaws me like a burning worm. And I

do not have the enjoyment which I was promised

Keep in mind the misery of this man, and may it be an everlasting caution to you.

Well, this is fearful. God holds me to watch and be sober, and to pray that I may shun the cause of this man's misery.

Then Christian was led into a chamber.

85

The Dream of Judgment

In the morning of the following day, he was again led into a room to watch a man rise from the bed. As he put on his raiment, he shook and trembled.

What's wrong with you, man?

Oh, I just had a dream! Behold, the heavens became dark, and there were fearful thunders and lightening.

The clouds moved at an unusual speed. A trumpet sounded and a man appeared sitting on a cloud.

Attended by thousands of heavenly beings; they were all in flaming fire.

At the command of that man, the rocks split, the graves opened, and the dead that were there came forth.

The man that sat upon the cloud opened a big book and bid the world draw near.

Rev. 20:11-14

Some of them were glad, and looked upward.

Some of them tried to hide themselves under the mountains.

The bottomless pit opened up and smoke and fire came out of it.
Gather together the weeds, the chaff, and stubble, and throw them into the burning lake of fire.
Matt. 3:1; 13:30; 24:30
The man who sat upon the cloud still kept His eyes on me
"Gather the wheat into his garner!
I Thess. 4:16,17
Luke 3:17
At this, many were caught up and were carried away in the cloud, but I was left behind.
I thought that the Day of Judgment had come. Because I was not ready for it. This frightens me greatly.

CHRISTIAN REACHES THE CROSS

Now I saw in my dream that the highway on which Christian was going was fenced on either side with wall, and that wall was called Salvation. Isa. 26:1

At the top of a small hill, there stood the Cross, and a little below, near the bottom, was a sepulcher.

As he stood right in front of the Cross, his burden came loose from his shoulders and fell off his back.

The burden rolled down till it came to the mouth of the sepulcher, where it fell in, and I saw it no more.

He has given me rest by His sorrow and life by His death.

Now as he stood and wept, Zech. 12:10

three shining ones came to him, and saluted him saying;

Peace be to you.

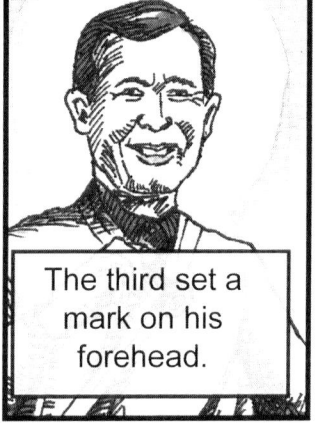

Simple, Sloth and Presumption

I saw then in my dream that he met three men sleeping by the roadside. Their names were Simple, Sloth and Presumption.

Men, you are like those who slept on the top of a mast, for the Dead Sea is under you, the gulf that has no bottom.

Awake, and come away, and I will help you off with your irons if you are willing.

I see no danger.

Yet, a little more sleep.

Every tub must stand on its own bottom.

They esteemed him so little that they neglected his proffering.

Formalist and Hypocrisy

Yes, Hypocrisy.

John 10:1

Why did you climb over the wall like a thief and a robber?

Hurry up to catch up with that man.

It was too far to go through the gate.

Therefore, we made a short cut of it as they had done.

But it was a trespassing against the Lord of heaven. You guys violated His revealed will.

Oh, come on! We didn't. We just took a short cut.

If we get into the way, what matter is it which way we get in. If we are in, we are in. It's become the law and the rule. By the way, you came through the gate. Is your condition better than ours?

I walk by the rule of my master. You come in by yourselves without his direction,

And you shall go out by yourselves without his mercy.

By law and ordinances you will not be saved, since you did not come in by the door.

Gal 2:16

Then Christian told them everything in detail about going through the gate till he met with the three shining men.

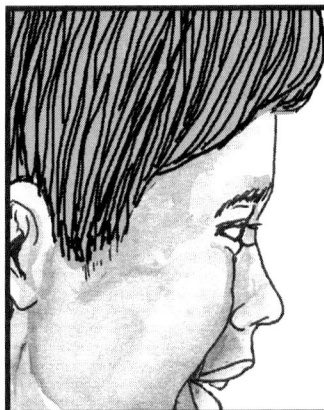

The Three Ways

Now they came to the foot of the hill Difficulty.

At the bottom there was a spring. And two other ways appeared as well.

The two ways were named Danger and Destruction.

Isa. 49: 10

Christian chose the difficult way that led up to the hill. He drank from the spring to refresh himself.

And then he began to go up the hill, saying

*"The hill though high,
I covet to ascend,
the difficulty
will not me offend..*

98

But when the other two came to the foothill and saw how steep and high the hill was, one chose the way to Danger and the other to Destruction.

They thought that they would meet with Christian again on the other side of the hill.

The way that Formalist took led him into a great wood.

Hypocrite, who took the way to Destruction,

was led into a wide field, full of dark mountains where he stumbled and fell. He rose no more.

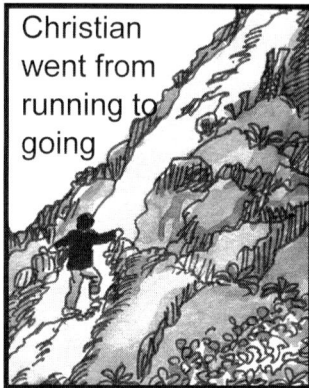

Christian went from running to going

and from going to clambering upon his hands and knees,

because the road was so steep,

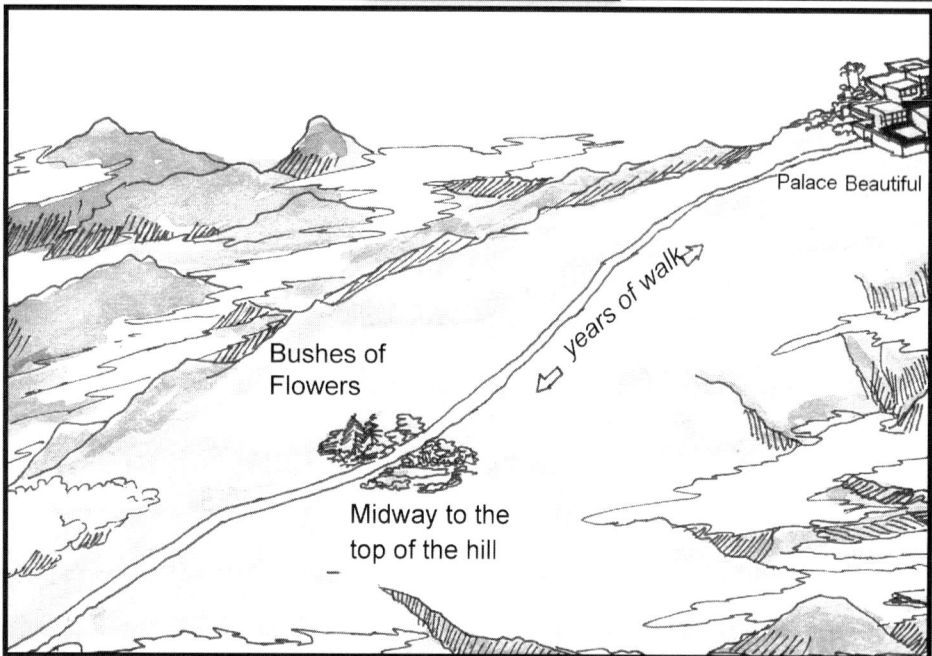

Palace Beautiful

years of walk

Bushes of Flowers

Midway to the top of the hill

THE PLEASANT ARBOR

Now about midway to the top of the hill there was located a pleasant arbor, for the refreshment of weary travelers.

The flowers were beautiful and the fragrance of them made Christian refreshed.

Christian took out his roll and read it to his comfort as he sat down. Awhile later, he fell asleep.

While he was in his sleep, the roll fell out of his hand. It was getting dark.

It was almost dark when someone came to him and woke him up, saying;

Go watch the ants, you lazy person. Watch what they do and be wise. Pro. 6:6

Christian then got up quickly and sped himself on his way, and did not stop till he came to the top of the hill.

The moment he got up to the top of the hill, there came two men running down to encounter him. They were Timorous and Mistrust.

Hey, hey run, run for your life.

We were going to the city of Zion, and we got up that difficult place.

But two lions lay in the way.

If we went closer, they would surely pull us to pieces.

How frightening it was to see such wild predators alive!

Yes, that's why we are going back.

To go back is nothing but death. To go forward is fear of death and ever lasting life is beyond it. I will yet go forward.

The two ran down the hill, but Christian went on his way.

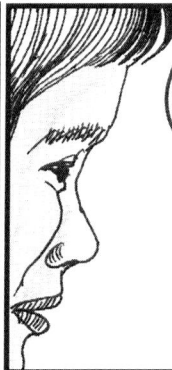

Well, I'd better read to encourage myself for awhile.

He felt in his bosom for the roll, but he found it not.

Oh my goodness, where did I drop it! On the way or at the Arbor!

He blamed himself for being so foolish to fall asleep in that place.

Oh, how foolish I was.

He turned back and ran down the hill to arbor to find his roll.

He felt so sorry that he wept.

He just realized how important it is to be alert and to have self-control.

At the beautiful Arbor, he looked for his roll around the place where he took a nap. There he found his roll at last. I Thess. 5:6-8

But who can tell how joyful he was when he found his roll again?

He tucked it into his bosom and resumed his way back up to the top of the hill again.

He thanked and praised God for finding his roll again.

It was really tiresome to go up the rest of the hill now.

He recalled what Mistrust and Timorous told him about the lions.

If I run into one of them in the dark how should I escape from getting torn to pieces?

Oh! You sinful sleeper, now you must walk without the sun.

Sometimes he sighed. Sometimes he chided himself as he went on his way up.

The Palace Beautiful

While he was bewailing his unhappy miscarriage, he lifted his eyes and looked. There was a very stately palace before him, which stood by the highway.

Rev. 3:2
I Thess. 5:7,8

Uh, the path has become really narrow!

Before him, there were two lions lying in the way.

The lions were both chained, but he did not see the chains.

Well, there's nothing but death before me. I'd better go back after those guys.

However, Porter happened to see Christian through the window.

Hey, are you so weak? Don't be afraid of the lions. They are chained.

Mark 4:40

and are placed there on the trail of faith.

My name is now Christian, though I was called Graceless before. May I lodge here tonight?

You are welcome. This house was built for the pilgrims like you. The Lord of the hill built it for the relief and security of pilgrims.

They can't harm you at all.

107

According to the rules of this house, she'll bring you into the rest of the family.

Well, I'll call out one of the virgins of this place.

So he rang the bell. Within a moment, a very beautiful, young lady came out to meet Christian. Her name was Discretion.

Then she started to ask him questions. Finally she asked his name. He answered all the questions.

After a little pause, she said,

So she smiled, but she held the tears in her eyes.

"I will call forth two or three more of my family.

She ran to the door and called out Prudence, Piety and Charity, who after a little more discourse with him, invited him into the family.

"Come in, you blessed man of the Lord. This house is built on purpose to entertain such pilgrims.

PIETY   **PRUDENCE**   **CHARITY**

He followed them into the house. When he got inside the house and sat down, they gave him something to drink.

Discourse with Piety

What moved you at first to a pilgrim's life?

I was driven out of my native country by a dreadful sound that was in my ears, that unavoidable destruction would come if I live in that place.

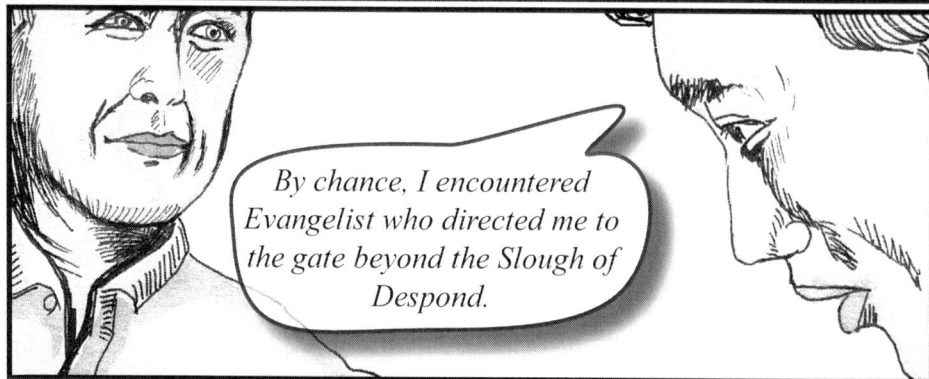

By chance, I encountered Evangelist who directed me to the gate beyond the Slough of Despond.

Did you not come by the house of Interpreter?

Yes, I did.

He has taught me well. I will remember his teachings as long as I live.

He also brought me to a stately palace,

where many people wearing golden clothes were.

There was a very adventurous man who fought through the armed guards outside the gate into the palace.

And then Christian told him about everything in detail beginning from the moment he was allowed into the Interpreter's house to the end.

...and that man told me his dream of the judgment day..

And what else did you see in the way?

I saw the Cross, a wooden cross, as I thought in my mind; there hung bleeding Lord, and very sight of him made my burden fall off my back.

Discourse with Prudence
Now began a serious discussion with Prudence.
Have you not been homesick often?
Yes, I had been a little at first, but with much shame and detestation.
However, now I desire a better country that is a heavenly one.
Heb. 11:15,16
Do you not yet bear away with you some of the things that then you were conversant with?
Yes, but...

Greatly against my will, especially my inward and carnal cognition, with which all men as well as myself were delighted.

But I chose my own things, that I would never think of those things any more,. However, I learned this, when I want to do good, evil is there with me. Rom. 7:15-21

Do you not find sometimes as if those things were vanquished, which at other times are your perplexity?

Yes, but that's seldom, and they are to me golden hours in which such things happen to me.

Can you remember by what means you find your annoyances at times as if they were overcome?

Yes, when I think what I saw at the Cross, whenever I looked at my embroidered coat, and also when I read the roll that I carry in my bosom.

What is it that makes you so desirous to go to mount Zion?

Because I know that when I get there, he will wipe away every tear from my eyes, and there'll be no more pain, death or sadness.

Rev. 21:4

Discourse with Charity

Don't you have a family?

Yes I do. I have a wife and four small children.

My heart was broken when I realized that they were not coming along with me.

No matter how many times I told them what God had shown to me of the destruction of our city, they didn't believe me at all.

They just mocked me and they thought I was crazy.

Gen. 19:14

117

SERIOUS DISCUSSION at SUPPER

They were talking together until supper was ready.

They enjoyed eating delicacies and drinking the finest wine. All they talked about at the dinning table was about the Lord of the hill.

About what he had done, where he lived and what he did, why he had built this house and so on.

He did it with the loss of much blood. However, which put the glory of grace into all,

as they say, and I believe that

He did it out of pure love to this country.

He had made many Pilgrims princes and princesses though by nature they were born beggars and their original abode had been dunghill.
I Sam. 2:8; Ps 113:7

He's such a lover of poor pilgrims that the like is not to be found on this earth.

Thus, they talked, discussing seriously till late at night.

After a night prayer was said together, they gave Christian a large upper chamber.

The Chamber of Peace

When the day broke, Christian got up from his bed and sang in the chamber of peace.

Where am I now? Is this the love and care of Jesus, for the men that pilgrims are?

In the morning, after some more discourse, they started to show him the rarities of that place.

They led him into the study.

They showed him records of the greatest antiquity; the pedigree of the Lord of the hill

The records said that He was the Son of the Ancient of days, and came by an eternal generation.

The names of many hundreds that he had taken into His services;

Heb. 11:33, 34

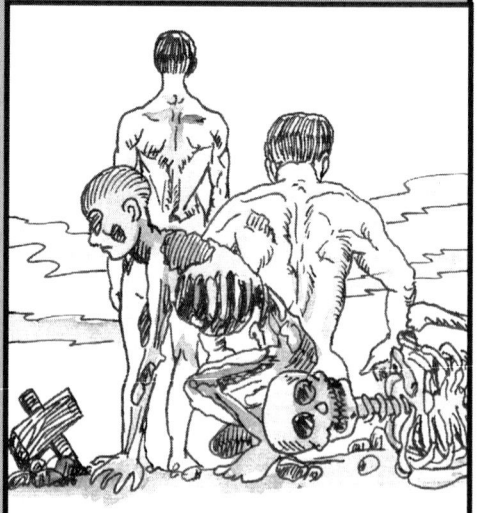

about those heroes of faith.

all were indeed the comfort and solace of pilgrims.

The
ARMORY

On the second day, they took him into the armory.

The armor that is provided for pilgrims;

helmet,

sword

shield

breast-plate

shoes that would not wear out.

prayer books

hammer and nails of Joel

pitchers and trumpet and lamp of Gideon

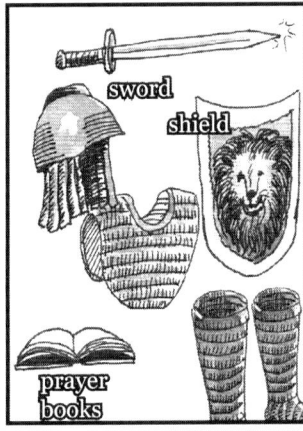

They also showed him those weapons that heroes in the Old Testament time used to defeat their enemies.

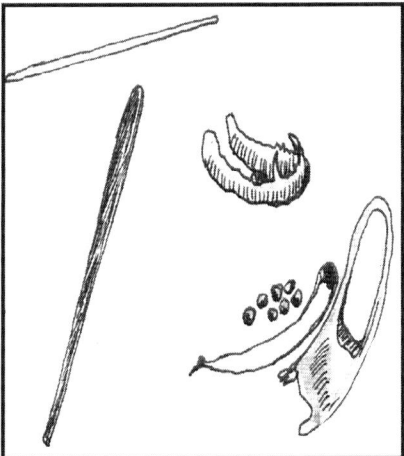

Ox's goad of Shamgar

Moses' rod

The jawbone which Samson used

the sling and the stones of little David, the King

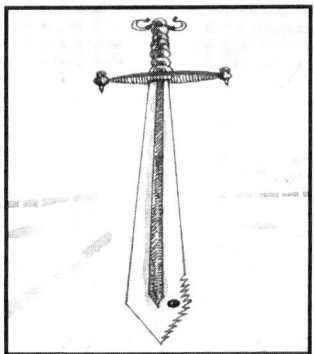

The Sword of God which will be used on the judgment day.

After this, they all went to sleep again. It was the third night that he was there.

They showed him many other excellent things besides. Christian was much delighted.

The third day morning, they brought him to the top of the house and bid him look south.

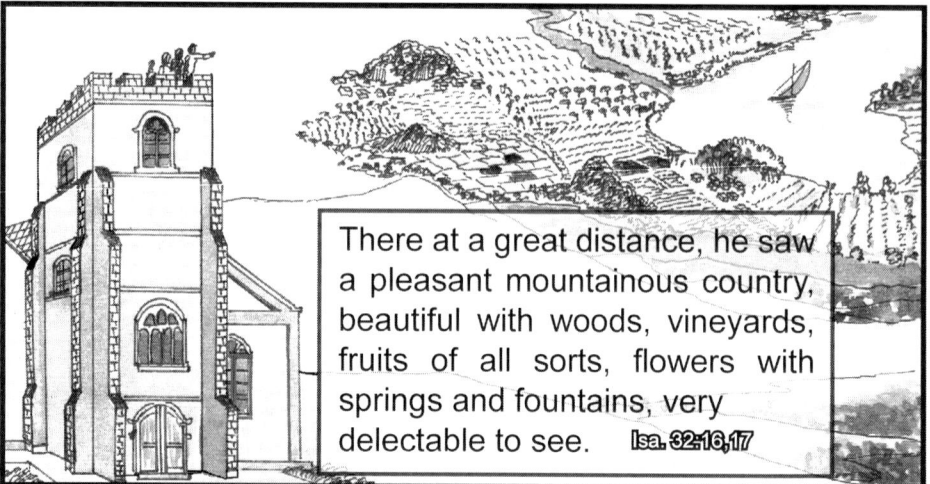

There at a great distance, he saw a pleasant mountainous country, beautiful with woods, vineyards, fruits of all sorts, flowers with springs and fountains, very delectable to see. Isa. 32:16,17

They said it was Immanuel's Land.

It is as common as this hill is, to and for all the pilgrims.

You may see from there, to the gate of the celestial city.

They accompanied him down to the foothill.

Now, Christian, it is a hard matter for a man to go down into the valley of humiliation.

Thank you so much.

Take these; a loaf of bread, a bottle of wine, and a cluster of raisins.

Then they went back to their place as Christian continued his journey.

Christian meets Apollyon

But now in the valley of humili-ation........

After a time of walking alone, he saw a foul fiend coming over the field to meet him. His name was Apollyon. Now Christian be-gan to be very afraid.

Oh my God! What a monster is that?

Now the beast was hideous to see. He was clothed with scales like a fish, wings like a dragon, feet like a bear. It had a lion's mouth and from its belly came out fire and smoke!

Pilgrim's Progress
Part II & III

Story Written by

John Bunyan

Illustrated by

James Tung
(a Lisu Refugee from Myanmar)

Edwards Brothers,Inc!
Thorofare, NJ 08086
4 March, 2011
A2011063

Edwards Brothers,Inc!
Thorofare, NJ 08086
04 March, 2011
BA2011063